DANNY'S BIRTHDAY

Mike Dickinson

Little
Hippo

When Danny woke up on this birthday,
he saw a big pile of presents.

This Little Hippo
book belongs to

Daniel Taylor Wright

Scholastic Children's Books,
Commonwealth House, 1-19 New Oxford Street
London WC1A 1NU, UK
a division of Scholastic Ltd

London • New York • Toronto • Sydney • Auckland
Mexico City • New Delhi • Hong Kong

First published in the UK in 2000 by Little Hippo, an imprint of Scholastic Ltd

ISBN 0 439 01191 4

Printed and bound in Italy

2 4 6 8 10 9 7 5 3 1

He leapt out of bed and ripped off
all the wrapping paper.

"You must write and thank everyone
for your presents, Danny," said Mummy.

He had . . .

cartoon stickers,

a football kit,

a pair of goldfish,

a snorkel and
swimming mask,

some toffees,

and a tent.

But Danny had unwrapped
his presents in such a hurry,
he could not remember
who had sent them.
"I'll have to guess,"
he said.

Now cousin Wayne is a footballer.

He must have sent the
football kit, thought Danny.

And Great Uncle Mike is a cartoonist . . .

He must have sent
the cartoon stickers.

Granny has a sweet shop . . .

So the toffees must
have come from her.

Aunt Lucy is a vet.

She is sure to have sent
the goldfish.

The snorkel and swimming mask came from cousin Ryan, the lifeguard.

And, of course, Aunt Fiona spends her time travelling around the world.

So she must have sent the tent.

The postman delivered all Danny's letters.

"I hope you didn't forget to thank Grandad" said Mummy.

But Danny had forgotten. He could not remember which present Grandad had sent. He wrote a thank you letter all the same and delivered it himself.

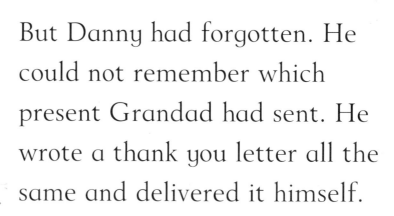

When cousin Wayne, the footballer, read
Danny's letter, he had an awful shock.

"Thank you for the present,"
wrote Danny. "I will always
put them on when I play football."

But cousin Wayne had sent Danny the cartoon stickers.

"How silly," he said. "Playing football with cartoon stickers all over him. I'll go and see his mother at once."

Great Uncle Mike, the cartoonist, groaned when he read Danny's letter.

"Thank you for the present," wrote Danny. "I licked them all and stuck them in an album."

But Great Uncle Mike had sent Danny
the toffees.

"Stupid boy," he said. "Sticking
my toffees in an album.
I'll go and see his
mother at once."

When Granny, who has the sweet shop, read Danny's letter, she felt sick.

"Thank you for the present," wrote Danny. "They last a long time if you suck them slowly."

But Granny had sent the goldfish!

"How dreadful," she said,
"He's sucking my goldfish!
I'll go and see his
mother at once."

"Oh dear," said Aunt Lucy, the vet, when she read Danny's letter.

"Thank you for the present," wrote Danny. "I'm getting a fish tank for them."

But Aunt Lucy had sent the snorkel
and the swimming mask.

"He'll break his neck diving into a fish tank,"
she cried. "I'll go and see his mother at once."

"Wow!" said cousin Ryan, when he opened
Danny's letter.

"Thank you for the present,"
wrote Danny. "I can use
it at the bottom of
the sea."

But cousin Ryan had sent the tent.

"Man!" he said. "That's reckless. He's going to drown. I'll go and see his mother at once."

When Aunt Fiona read Danny's letter,
she gasped.

"Thank you for the
present," Danny wrote.
"Me and my friend are
going to sleep out in it."

But Aunt Fiona had sent the football kit.

"How absurd," she said. "Camping out
in a football kit. I'll go and see his
mother at once."

When Grandad opened Danny's letter,
he laughed and laughed.
"Thank you for the present," wrote Danny.
"I liked it best of all."

But Grandad had not given Danny his
present yet. It was still in the oven!
"I must take it round at once," he said.

Everyone arrived at Danny's house at the same time. Mummy heard the noise and opened the door. "What a muddle!" she laughed. "Come inside and we'll sort it all out."

When Danny explained what had happened,
everyone laughed. Grandad arrived with
the birthday cake.

"Thank you for the presents," smiled Danny.

"Happy Birthday, Danny!"
they all said.